VOYAGE AROUND MY ROOM

Xavier de Maistre

Translated from the French by Kristen Hall-Geisler

Translation by Kristen Hall-Geisler
Original title: *Voyage autour de ma chambre*
Translation copyright ©2020 by Practical Fox

ISBN 978-1-7320603-5-7

de Maistre, Xavier
Voyage Around My Room

Practical Fox, LLC
Portland, Oregon
www.practicalfox.com

Note from the Translator

I HAVE ADDED REFERENCES TO the text that a modern North American audience might not know offhand, like the names of plays or brief biographical information for names used. I have also used modern US dialogue style conventions, such as quotation marks and new lines for new speakers.

Chapter 1

I T IS SO GLORIOUS TO embark on a new career and to appear all of a sudden in the scholarly world with a book of discoveries in one's hand, like an unexpected comet glittering through space!

I will not hold my book "in petto," or secret. Here it is, everyone—read. I undertook and completed a forty-two-day voyage around my room.

The interesting observations that I made and the constant pleasures that I experienced along the way made me think I should make this public. The certainty of being helpful decided it for me.

I feel an inexpressible satisfaction in my heart when I think of the infinite number of unfortunates to whom I offer a resource that's guaranteed not to be boring and instead be a sweetening of the evils they endure.

The pleasure that one finds in voyaging in one's room is a refuge from the anxious jealousy of men; it is independent of fortune.

Is there any being, in truth, so unhappy, so abandoned, the he doesn't have a little room where he can retire and hide himself from the world? Here everything is prepared for the voyage.

I'm sure that all men of sense will adopt my system, no matter what their character may be, or what temperament. Be he miser or spendthrift, rich or poor, young or old, born in the tropics or near the pole, he could travel like me. In the boundless family of men that teems on the earth's surface, there is not a soul—no, not a soul (I mean, of those who live in rooms)—who can, after having read this book, withhold his approval of this new manner of travel that I introduce to the world.

CHAPTER 2

I COULD BEGIN THE ELEGY of my voyage by saying that it didn't cost me anything. This fact merits attention. This will be endorsed and celebrated by people of moderate wealth. There is another class of men for whom this is surer still to be a happy success, and for the same reason: that it costs nothing. "And who might they be?" What! You have to ask? It's rich people. Moreover, what resources do the sick need for this kind of travel? There's no need at all to fear the intemperance of the air or seasons. Cowards will be sheltered from thieves; they'll meet neither precipices nor potholes. Thousands of people who before me didn't dare, others who couldn't, and still others who haven't even dreamed of travel will decide to go using my example. Would the laziest being in the world hesitate to set out with me on a route to find pleasure when it doesn't cost him anything?

Then take heart! Let's embark.

Follow me, all of you for whom the pangs of love or a negligence of friendship keeps you in your apartment, far from the pettiness and perfidy of men.

May all the sad, the sick, and the bored in the world follow me! May all the sluggish get up en masse! And you who roll sinister projects of reform around in your minds or retreat due to some infidelity; you who, from your bedroom, renounce the world for the rest of your life; amiable anchoress of an evening, you come too.

Believe me—leave behind these dark ideas. You lose an instant of pleasure without gaining one for wisdom. Be so good as to accompany me on a voyage. We will walk on our little journey, laughing along the way, as travelers who have seen Rome and Paris. No obstacle can stop us, and giving ourselves gaily over to our imagination, we will follow it wherever it wants to lead us.

CHAPTER 3

THERE ARE SO MANY CURIOUS people in the world!

I was persuaded that the curious would like to know why my voyage around my room takes forty-two days rather than forty-three, or some other length of time. But how can I tell the reader this, seeing that I don't know myself? All I can say for sure is that if the work is too long for your taste, it wasn't my responsibility to make it shorter. All vanity of the traveler aside, I would have been happy with one chapter. I was, it's true, in my room with all possible pleasure and agreeableness. But alas! I was not the master of my ability to voluntarily leave here. I even think that, without the intervention of certain powerful persons who took an interest in me, and for whom my gratitude is undimmed, I would have had time to bring one entire folio to light—so much were the guards who made me travel in my room disposed in my favor.

Meanwhile, reasonable reader, see how wrong these men were, and grasp, if you can, the logic that I am about to present to you.

Is anything more natural and more just than to cut the throat of someone who stepped on your foot by accident? Or who let slip an offensive term in a moment of pique caused by your own imprudence? Or who has the misfortune to be liked by your mistress?

You go into a meadow and there, like Nicole in Molière's *Le Bourgeois Gentilhomme*, you try to draw the fourth cut when your opponent parries tierce, and so that vengeance may be sure and complete, you show to him your exposed chest, running the risk of being killed by your enemy to avenge yourself. You see that nothing is more important, yet you find people who disapprove of this laudable custom!

But what is more important than all the rest is that these same people who disapprove of the custom and who want us to regard it as a serious fault will treat yet more badly those who refuse to practice. Many an unhappy soul, in conforming himself to this opinion, has lost his reputation and his employment. So when you have the bad luck to have what they call an "affair of honor," you wouldn't do badly to draw lots to find out if it will be finished following the letter of the law or its use. As the laws and their usage are contradictory, the judges would also be able to roll the dice for their sentence.

And it's also probably because of a decision like this that it's necessary to explain why and how my voyage lasted exactly forty-two days.

Chapter 4

MY ROOM IS SITUATED AT 45 degrees latitude, according to the measurements of Father Beccaria; its orientation is from sunrise to sunset; it forms a long square that has thirty-six steps from wall to wall. My voyage will be considerably longer, because I will traverse it often in length and width or even diagonally without following a plan or method. I might even make zigzags. And I will travel all the lines possible in geometry if need be.

I don't like people who are very strict masters of their steps and their ideas, who say, "Today I will make three visits, I will write four letters, I will finish this project that I began." My soul is so open to all sorts of ideas, tastes, and sentiments; it eagerly receives all that come before it.

And why would my soul refuse the pleasures that are so sparse on this difficult path of life? They are so rare, and so scattered, that you'd have to be crazy not to stop or even leave your path to gather up all those things within our reach.

There's nothing more appealing, I think, than to follow one's ideas along the trail, like the hunter pursuing prey, without pretending to hold to any particular route. Also, while I travel in my room, I rarely wander in a straight line. I go from my table to a painting hung in a corner. From there I start off obliquely toward the door. But although my intention when I set off may well be to arrive at the door, if I encounter my armchair along my route, I don't make it all the way, and I quickly make myself comfortable.

It's an excellent piece of furniture, an armchair. It is above all of the utmost utility for meditative men. In the long evenings of winter, it is sometimes nice, and always prudent, to stretch out gently there, far from the fracas of large crowds. A good fire, books, pens: what reserves against boredom! And there's still more pleasure in forgetting the books and pens to poke the fire, abandoning yourself to some sweet thought or composing some rhymes to cheer up your friends. The hours glide by for you then and fall silently into eternity, without your feeling their sad passage.

CHAPTER 5

AFTER MY ARMCHAIR, WALKING TOWARD the north, we discover my bed, which is placed at the rear of my room, creating the most agreeable perspective. It is situated in the most pleasant manner: the first rays of the sun come to play on my bed curtains. I watch them, in the lovely days of summer, advance the length of the white wall as they trace the sun's rise. The elms that are in front of my window divide the rays a million ways and make them sway on my rose-and-white bed, scattering the charming tint of their reflection all around. I hear the confused chirping of the swallows that are perched on the roof of the house, and a thousand merry ideas occupy my mind. In the whole universe, no one's awakening is so agreeable, so peaceful, as mine.

I admit that I love to indulge these sweet moments and that I always prolong, as often as possible, the pleasure that I find in thinking while in the comfortable warmth of my bed. Is this a theater that readies my imagination, that awakens the most tender ideas, this piece of furniture where I sometimes forget myself? Modest reader, don't be alarmed, but could I not then speak of the happiness of a lover who holds in his arms for the first time a virtuous spouse? An ineffable pleasure that my unlucky destiny condemns me never to taste! Is it not in a bed that a mother, drunk on the joy after the birth of a son, forgets her woes? It's there that fantastic pleasures, fruits of imagination, and dreams come to shake us.

It's in this delicious furniture that we forget, for half of our life, the worries of the other half. But what a crowd of agreeable and sad thoughts press at once in my mind—an astonishing mélange of terrible and delectable situations!

A bed sees our births and our deaths. It's the ever-changing theater where the human story plays out over and over, round and round—the intriguing dramas, the ridiculous farces, and the terrible tragedies. It's a crib adorned with flowers; it's the throne of love; it's a sepulcher.

Chapter 6

THIS CHAPTER IS ABSOLUTELY ONLY for meta-physicians. I'm going to shine brightest daylight onto the nature of man. It's the prism with which you can analyze and break down the freedoms of men by separating animal power from rays of pure intelligence.

It seems to me impossible to explain how and why I burned my fingers during the first steps I took in beginning this voyage without explaining in great detail to the reader my system of the soul and the jackass. This metaphysical discovery so influences my ideas and my actions that it will be very difficult to understand this book if I don't give the key at the outset.

I realized, through many observations, that man

is composed of a soul and a jackass. These two beings are absolutely distinct, but so embodied in the other—or one inside the other—that the soul has to have a certain superiority over the jackass in order to even be able to make the distinction.

I heard from an old professor (from as long ago as I can remember) that Plato called this substance "the other." That's all well and good, but I would prefer to give this name par excellence to the jackass that is joined to our soul. It's really this substance that is "the other" and that plays strange tricks on us. We can plainly see that man has a double nature, but they say this is because he is composed of a soul and a body. They accuse this body of I don't know how many things, but they go about it very badly, because the body is incapable of conscious thought. It's the jackass that must take the fall, this sensitive being, which is truly individual in that it has its own separate existence, its tastes, its inclinations, its will. It is not below other animals because it is educated and equipped with perfect organs.

Ladies and gentlemen, be proud of your intelligence if it makes you happy, but defy "the other" often, above all when you are together.

I have performed I don't know how many tests on the union of these two heterogenous creatures. For example, I have clearly recognized that the soul can be made to obey the jackass and that, in retaliation, this same jackass very often obliges the soul to get riled up against its will. According to the rules, one has legislative power and the other executive power, but these two powers are often contrary. The great art of a genius is to know how to educate his jackass until it is able to go it alone while the soul, released from this tedious acquaintance, raises itself toward the heavens.

But I need to clarify this with an example.

When you read a book and a most interesting idea strikes your imagination, your soul quickly latches onto it and forgets about the book while your eyes mechanically follow the words and lines. You finish the page without understanding it and without remembering what you read. This is because your soul has ordered its companion to keep on reading but doesn't alert you at all to its absence. "The other" continued the reading that your soul no longer heard.

CHAPTER 7

IS IT NOT CLEAR TO you? Here's another example.
One day last summer, I went to court. I had
painted all morning, and my soul, being happy
to meditate on the painting, left the evening to the
jackass to transport me to the king's palace.

Painting is a sublime art! thought my soul, pleased that
the spectacle of nature had been touched upon,
that I wasn't obliged to make a living through painting, that I don't only paint to pass the time but,
stricken by the majesty of a lovely face and the admi-
rable play of light that deepens the shades of a human
face a thousand times, I attempt to approach in these
works the sublime effects of nature.

Happier still is the painter who is followed by his
love of the countryside on his solo walks, who knows

how to express on canvas the feeling of sadness, who is inspired by a somber wood or empty field. These works imitate and reproduce nature. The work creates new seas and dark caverns unknown to the sun. The green groves spring from nothingness; the blue of the sky is reflected in the paintings. The painter knows the art of stirring the air and making the tempest howl.

Other times he offers to the eye of the enchanted viewer the rich countryside of ancient Sicily. You can see the wild, fleeting nymphs traversing the reeds to chase a satyr. The temples of a majestic architecture raise their grand facades above the sacred forest that surrounds them. Imagination gets lost in the silent paths of this ideal country. The distant blues mix with the sky, and the entire countryside, echoing in the waters of a tranquil stream, forms a spectacle that no language can describe.

While my soul made these reflections, "the other" went its way, and God knows where it went! Instead of going to the court, as it had been told to do, it veered so far to the left that at the moment where my soul caught it again, it was at the door of Madame de Hautcastel, a half mile from the royal palace.

I leave to the reader's imagination what would have occurred if "the other" had entered the house of such a good woman all alone.

CHAPTER 8

IF IT'S USEFUL AND AGREEABLE to have a soul disengaged from the material realm, to the point of traveling alone when it's appropriate, this ability is also inconvenient. It's because of this, for example, that I burned myself, which I spoke of in the previous chapter. I usually give my jackass the courtesy of preparing my lunch; it's the one who toasts my bread and cuts it into slices. It makes a marvelous coffee, and quite often does so without my soul getting mixed up in the process—unless my soul is amusing itself in watching "the other" work, but that's rare and difficult to make happen. It's easy, when you do some mechanical operation, to think of other things, but it's extremely difficult to watch yourself work. Or, to explain myself by following my system, it's difficult to use the soul to examine the work of the jackass and watch it without taking part. This is the most astonishing metaphysical tour de force that man can execute.

I rested my tongs on the embers to toast my bread, and some time later, while my soul traveled, a flaming log rolled out onto the hearth. My poor jackass grabbed the tongs, and I burned my fingers.

CHAPTER 9

I HOPE TO HAVE SUFFICIENTLY developed my ideas in the preceding chapters to give the reader something to think about and to prepare him at the same time to make discoveries on this brilliant route. The reader can only satisfy himself if he reaches a day where he knows how to send his soul on a voyage all alone. The pleasures that this ability brings him will balance the rest of the mistakes that could result. Is there a pleasure more flattering than that of stretching your existence in this way, across time and earth and heavens, and doubling, so to speak, your very being? Isn't it the eternal desire and lack of satisfaction in man that augment his strengths and his faculties to want to be where he isn't, to recall the past and live in the future?

He wants to command armies, preside over academies; he wants to be adored by beautiful women; and if he possesses all of that, then he misses the fields and the tranquility and transfers his longing to the shepherd's cabin. His projects, his hopes, unceasingly fail against the real miseries attached to human nature. He will not find happiness there. A fifteen-minute voyage with me will show him the way.

Ah! Why does he not leave to "the other" these miserable cares, this ambition that torments him? Come, you poor, unfortunate soul! Make an effort to break out of your prison. From the heights of heaven where I'm going to lead you, the place of celestial spheres, look to your jackass, tossed into the world to run along the path toward fortune and honor all alone. See with what gravity it walks among men. The crowd parts with respect, and believe me, no one will see that it is on its own. That's the last thing any crowd it walks among would suspect—knowing whether it has a soul with it or not, if it thinks or not. A thousand sentimental women will love it passionately without realizing there's no soul. The jackass can even raise itself, without the help of your soul, to the highest favor and the grandest fortune.

In the end, I would not be surprised at all if, on our return from the celestial sphere, your soul returns to your house and finds itself inside the jackass of a great lord.

Chapter 10

YOU MUST NOT BELIEVE THAT I'm not keeping my word in giving the description of my voyage around my room, that I am beating around the bush to get out of this matter. You'll find my word good because my voyage actually continues, during which time my soul, withdrawing into itself, ranged in the preceding chapter across the twisting metaphysical detours.

I had seated myself in my armchair, and I positioned it so that its two front feet were lifted two inches from the ground. Then, while tipping left and right and gaining ground, I slowly made my way to the wall. (That's how I travel when I'm not pressed for time.)

There, one hand automatically seized the portrait

of Madame de Hautcastel, and "the other" amused itself in cleaning the dust that covered the frame. This task gave my jackass a peaceful pleasure, and this pleasure was felt in my soul, although it was lost in the vast expanse of the heavens. It is good to observe that when the spirit of travel is thus in space, it always keeps a hold on sense by some kind of secret so that without disrupting its occupations, it could take part in the peaceful pleasures of "the other." But if this pleasure grows to a certain point, or if it's struck by some unexpected spectacle, the soul soon enough retreats to its proper place with the speed of lightning.

That's what came to me when I cleaned the portrait.

To the extent that the cloth removed the dust and made the blond curls appear, as well as the garland of roses with which they are crowned, my soul, from the sun where it had transported itself, felt a light shudder of pleasure and shared sympathetically the happiness in my heart. This joy became less muddled and more vivid when the cloth, with a single swipe, revealed the bright mien of this charming face. My soul was on the verge of leaving the heavens to enjoy this sight.

But had it found itself in the Elysian Fields assisted by a choir of cherubim, it could not have stayed even half a second when its companion, taking all the more interest in the work, grabbed a damp sponge that was held out to it and passed it all at once over the eyelashes and eyes—over the nose—over the cheeks—over this mouth—ah God! my heart beats—over the chin—over the breast.

This was the matter of a moment. The entire figure seemed reborn and sprang from nothingness. My soul dropped from the sky like a falling star. It found "the other" in a state of ecstasy and elevated it by sharing this feeling.

This singular and unforeseen situation dispelled time and space for me. I existed for an instant in the past and was rejuvenated against the laws of nature. Yes, there she is, this adored woman; it's her. I see her smiling. She's going to speak to say she loves me. What a gaze! Come that I may hold you to my heart, soul of my life, my second self! Come share my rapture and my happiness!

This moment was short, but it was ravishing. Cold reason soon returned to its empire, and in the blink of an eye, I had aged a whole year. My heart became cold, icy, and I found myself once again with the crowd of apathetic people who weigh down the world.

Chapter 11

W̲E̲ ̲D̲O̲N̲'̲T̲ ̲N̲E̲E̲D̲ ̲T̲O̲ ̲J̲U̲M̲P̲ ahead; my eagerness to communicate to the reader my system of the soul and the jackass made me abandon the description of my bed sooner than I should have. I shall take up my voyage where I interrupted it in the previous chapter. I only ask you recall that we left half of myself holding the portrait of Madame de Hautcastel near the wall, four steps from my desk.

I had forgotten, in speaking of my bed, to recommend to all who are able to have one a rose-and-white bed: it is certain that these colors influence us, cheer us up or bring us down, according to their shades. Rose and white are two colors recognized for pleasure and ease. Nature, in giving us the rose, gave us the crown of the floral empire. And when the sky wants to announce a beautiful day to the world, it colors the clouds this charming tint to raise the sun.

One day we were climbing with difficulty along a steep trail. The friendly Rosalie was in front; her agility gave her wings. We could not follow her. All of a sudden, arriving at the summit of a rise, she turned toward us to catch her breath and laughed at our slowness. Never have these two colors that I praise had this kind of triumph: her cheeks inflamed, her lips in coral, teeth gleaming, her alabaster throat over the deep green all around, striking to everyone's gaze. We must stop to contemplate her; I don't say anything of her blue eyes, nor the glance she threw us, because I would stray from my subject. Otherwise, I think of her as little as possible. It's enough for me to have given the loveliest example imaginable of the superiority of these two colors over all the others and of their influence over the happiness of men.

I will not go farther today. What subject could I take up that isn't insipid? What idea is not erased by this thought? I don't even know when I could set myself to work again. If I continue and the reader wants to see it through to the end, then he should address himself to the angel in charge of thoughts and ask him to no longer mix in the image of this rise among the thoughts that he constantly tosses my way.

Without this precaution, it's over for my voyage.

Chapter 12

.... the rise ....
....
....

CHAPTER 13

OUR EFFORTS ARE IN VAIN. I must stay here where I left off despite myself. It's a rest stop.

Chapter 14

I said that I especially love to meditate in the sweet warmth of my bed and that its lovely color greatly contributes to the pleasure I find in it.

For me to procure this pleasure, my butler has received the order to enter into my room a half hour before the time I plan to get up. I hear him lightly walk and discreetly rummage about in my room, and this noise gives me the joy of feeling myself doze—a delicate pleasure unknown to many people. You're awake enough to perceive that you're not awake entirely and to confusedly calculate that the time for business and boredom is still in the hourglass.

My man becomes imperceptibly noisier. It is so difficult for him to constrain himself; besides, he knows that the fatal hour approaches. He looks at my watch and rattles its chain to warn me, but I turn a deaf ear to further prolong this magical hour. It's not the kind of squabble I wish to have with this poor man. I have a hundred preliminary requests to give him to buy myself some time. He knows very well that these orders, which I give him in a bad mood, are only excuses for staying in bed without seeming to want to. He pretends not to know this, and I truly appreciate this.

Finally, when I've gathered all my resources, he moves to the middle of my room and stands there, his arms crossed, with the most perfect immobility. It's a fact that it's not possible to disapprove of my thoughts with more spirit and discretion; also, I never resist this unspoken invitation. I extend my arms to show him that I understand, and there I sit.

If the reader reflects on the conduct of my butler, you could convince yourself that, in certain delicate affairs of this sort, his simplicity and good sense are worth infinitely more than the most adroit mind. I dare to assert that the most studied discourse on the inconvenience of laziness would not get me out of bed more promptly than the mute reproach of Monsieur Joannetti.

He's a perfectly honest man, is Monsieur Joannetti, and the best-suited of all men for a traveler like me. He is accustomed to the frequent voyages of my soul and never laughs at the thoughtlessness of "the other." He even sometimes guides it when it is alone, so you could say then that "the other" is guided by two souls. When the jackass gets dressed, for example, Joannetti warns me with a signal that it is on the point of putting my stockings on backward, or the coat before the vest. My soul is often amused to see the poor Joannetti running after the madman under the arbor of the citadel to tell the jackass it forgot its hat or its handkerchief.

One day (will I warn the jackass?), without this loyal servant who catches it at the bottom of the stairs, the scatterbrain will make its way toward the court without its sword as boldly as the grand master of ceremonies carrying a majestic baguette.

CHAPTER 15

"Wait, Joannetti," I said to him, "hang this portrait." He had helped me clean it and no more suspected what had produced the portrait chapter than what happens on the moon. It was he who, of his own volition, presented me with the damp sponge and who, while appearing indifferent to my process, made it possible for my soul to travel to a hundred thousand places in an instant. Instead of putting the portrait back in its place, he had kept it to clean on his rounds.

A difficulty, a problem to solve, gave him an air of curiosity that I noted. "Let's see," I said to him. "What do you find fault with in this portrait?"

"Oh, nothing, sir!"

"And yet?"

He set it up on one of the shelves of my desk, then took a few steps back. "I would like," he said, "for monsieur to explain to me why this portrait always looks at me no matter where in the room I find myself. This morning, when I made the bed, her face turned toward me, and if I went to the window, she still looked at me and followed me with her eyes the whole way."

"In such a way, Joannetti," I said to him, "that if the room were full of people, this beautiful woman would watch everyone from all sides all the time?"

"Oh! Yes, monsieur."

"She would smile at all and sundry as she does me?"

Joannetti didn't answer.

I stretched out in my chair, and lowering my head, I gave myself over to more serious meditations. What a bright idea! Poor lover! While you languish far from your mistress, who might have already replaced you; while you avidly fix your gaze on her portrait and imagine yourself (at least as its painter) to be the sole observer; the perfidious effigy, as unfaithful as the original, bestows her gaze over all who surround her and smiles at everyone!

There is a resemblance in morality between certain portraits and their models that no philosopher, no painter, no observer has yet perceived.

I travel from discovery to discovery.

CHAPTER 16

JOANNETTI WAS STILL IN THE same position, waiting for the explanation he'd asked for. I raised my head from the folds of my traveling clothes, where I had settled in to meditate at my ease and to again go over the sad reflections that I came here to think about.

"Do you not see, Joannetti?" I said to him after a moment of silence and turning sideways in my chair. "Do you not see that the painting, being planar, bounces rays of light from every point of its surface?"

Joannetti, at this explanation, opened his eyes so wide that I could see all of his pupils, and his mouth hung open. These two movements in the human body announce, according to the famous painter Le Brun, the final stage of astonishment. The jackass, without a doubt, had undertaken a similar topic. My soul would know of the rest, of which Joannetti was completely unaware: what the surface of a plane is and, moreover, what rays of light are. At the prodigious widening of his eyes, I came back to myself and remembered my head was sunk into the collar of my traveling clothes. I stuck myself there so well that I succeeded in hiding my face almost entirely.

I resolved to eat lunch right here. The morning was very far along; one step more in my room would have brought my lunch into night. I slid up to the edge of my chair and, setting both feet on the hearth, I waited patiently for my meal. It's a comfortable position. It would be, I think, very difficult to find another that combines such advantages and that is also convenient for the inevitable stopovers of a long voyage.

Rosine, my faithful little dog, never misses coming over to tug the hems of my traveling clothes so that I'll put her in my lap. She finds a bed all arranged and very comfortable at the crux of the angle that forms the two parts of my body: a letter V represents my situation marvelously. Rosine rushes toward me if I don't pick her up as quickly as she likes. I often find her in my lap without knowing how she got there. My hands arrange themselves in the manner most favorable to her well-being.

Maybe there is sympathy between this amiable beast and my jackass; maybe that coincidence alone decided it. But I don't think it's coincidence at all, this sorry system. I would sooner think of Martinism, a form of Christian mysticism. No, I will never believe it.

There is one such reality in the rapport that exists between these two animals. When I set my feet on the hearth in pure distraction, when the dinner hour stretches on and I think nothing of taking a break, Rosine, alert to this movement, betrays her pleasure by slightly wagging her tail. Discretion keeps her in her place, and "the other," who perceives it, knows she likes it. Although incapable of figuring out what caused her happiness, it establishes between them a silent dialogue, a rapport of very good feelings that could absolutely not be attributed to coincidence.

Chapter 17

Don't reproach me for being prolix in the details; this is the way of travelers. When they take off to climb Mont Blanc, when they go visit the grand opening of the tomb of Empedocles, they never miss out on precisely describing the tiniest of circumstances: the number of people, the mules, the quality of the provisions, the excellent appetite of the travelers. All of it, including the typesetter's errors, is recorded in their journal for the instruction of the sedentary universe. By this principle, I resolved to speak of my dear Rosine, the friendly animal that I love with true affection, and to her I dedicate this entire chapter.

In the six years we have lived together, there has not been the least chill between us; or, if some small altercations arose, I swear in good faith that the fault has always been mine and that Rosine has always made the first step toward reconciliation.

One evening, when she was scolded, she went to bed sadly and without a whimper. The next day, at the crack of dawn, she was next to my bed in a respectful pose. At the least movement of her master, at the least sign of my waking, she announced her presence with the quick whapping of her tail against my night table.

And why would I refuse my affection to this affectionate being who has never stopped loving me ever since was started living together? I don't have room in my memory sufficient to enumerate all the people who were interested in me and then forgot me. I have had some friends, many mistresses, a crowd of affairs, still more acquaintances, and now I am no longer anything to anyone. They've even forgotten my name.

What protestations! What offers of help! I could count on their fortune, their eternal friendship, without reservation!

My dear Rosine, who has never offered me help at all, renders for me the greatest service that you can give to humanity: she loved me long ago, and she still loves me now. Also, I'm not at all afraid to say, I love her with the same kind of love that I give to my friends.

Let them say what they will.

CHAPTER 18

W E LEFT JOANNETTI IN HIS attitude of astonishment, standing immobile in front of me, waiting for the end of the sublime explanation that I had begun.

When he saw me suddenly sink into my dressing gown and from there finish my explanation, he didn't doubt for an instant that I was keeping it short for good reason and that he had consequently brought me low with this difficulty that he had proposed.

In spite of the physical superiority over me that he had acquired, he didn't feel the least movement of pride and didn't try at all to profit from his advantage. After a short moment of silence, he took the portrait, put it back in its place, and lightly retreated on tiptoe. He sensed that his presence was a kind of humiliation for me, and his propriety suggested to him that he should leave without my seeing him. His conduct on this occasion interested me very much, and his place in my heart rose further. He would have, without a doubt, a place in the heart of the reader. And if the reader is someone so insensitive to refuse this place to Joannetti after having read this chapter, heaven has certainly given you a heart of marble.

CHAPTER 19

"Dammit!" I said to Joannetti one day. "That's the third time that I told you to buy me a brush. What an airhead! What an ass!"

He didn't say a word. He hadn't answered the previous day either for a similar mistake.

"It's such a specific request!" I said. I didn't understand this at all. "Go look for a cloth to clean my boots," I said angrily.

As he left, I was sorry for having been so brusque. My wrath passed suddenly when I saw the care with which he was polishing and cleaning my boots. I pressed my hand to his shoulder in a sign of reconciliation.

What! I said to myself. *Are there men who clean mud from the boots of others for money?* This word *money* was like a beam of light that made things clear to me. I suddenly recalled that it had been a long time since I had given any to my butler.

"Joannetti," I said while retracting my feet, "do you have any money?"

A half smile of justification appeared on his lips at this question. "No, sir, for eight days I haven't had a cent. I spent all that was allotted to me for your little purchases."

"And the brush? It's surely for that?"

He still smiled. He could have said to his master, "No, I am not at all an airhead or an ass, as you so cruelly called your faithful butler. Pay me the twenty-three lires, ten sous, and four deniers that you owe me, and I will buy you your brush."

But he allowed the unjust abuse rather than cause his master to blush at his uncalled-for anger. What heavenly grace! Philosophers! Christians! Did you read that?

"Hold on, Joannetti," I said, "hold on, run out to buy the brush."

"But sir, do you want to stay like this with one clean boot and one filthy?"

"Go, I say, buy the brush. Leave this dirt on my boot."

He left. I took the cloth, and I happily cleaned my left boot, and I let fall a repentant tear.

Chapter 20

THE WALLS OF MY ROOM are decorated with prints and paintings that improve them significantly. I would like with all my heart for the reader to examine them one after the other to amuse and distract him on the long path that we are still to take to arrive at my desk. But is it just as impossible to clearly explain a painting as it is to create a portrait from a description.

What emotion wouldn't the reader feel, for example, in contemplating the first painting that presents itself for gazing! He would see there the unlucky Charlotte slowly wiping, with a trembling hand, Albert's pistols. Dark premonitions and all the anguish of love without hope or consolation are physically imprinted on her, while the icy Albert, surrounded by sacks of lawsuits and old papers of all kinds, turns coldly to wish his friend a bon voyage.

How many times was I tempted to break the glass that covers this print to pull this Albert from his table, to tear him to pieces, to trample him underfoot! But there will always be too many Alberts in this world. What is the sensitive man who doesn't have his own people with whom he is obliged to live and against whom the outpourings of his soul, the sweet emotions of his heart, and the flights of his imagination go to break like the tides on the rocks?

Happy is he who finds a friend with whom the heart and mind meet, a friend who is united with him by the same tastes, sentiments, and knowledge; a friend who is not tormented by ambition or interest, who prefers the shade of a tree to the pomp of a court! Happy is he who possesses a friend!

Chapter 21

I HAD ONE OF THOSE friends; death took him from me. It seized him at the beginning of his career, at the moment when his friendship was becoming a pressing need for my heart. We supported each other in the tiresome labors of war. We only had one pipe between us; we drank from the same cup; we slept under the same canvas; and in those miserable circumstances, the place where we lived together was for us a new homeland.

I saw him exposed to all the perils of war—of a disastrous war. Death seemed to save us for each other. A thousand times, it used up its spears without touching him, but this made his loss more touching for me. The tumult of arms, the enthusiasm that takes hold of the soul in the face of danger...maybe these could have prevented his cries from piercing my heart.

If his death were useful to his country and disastrous for his enemies, I would regret it less. But to lose him in the middle of the delights of our winter quarters! To see him die in my arms at the moment he appeared to overflow with health, at the moment where our friendship grew stronger still in peace and tranquility! Ah! I will never console myself. Nevertheless his memory lives only in my heart; it no longer exists among those who surrounded him and who replaced him. This idea makes the feeling of his loss more painful for me.

Nature, indifferent to the departure of individuals, again puts on her bright spring dress and adorns herself in all her beauty all around the cemetery where he lies. The trees cover themselves in leaves and interweave their branches; the birds sing in the foliage; the bugs buzz among the flowers; all breathe in joy and life in the home of the dead. And in the evening, while the moon shines in the sky and I meditate near this sad place, I hear the cricket happily carrying on with his never-ending song, hidden in the grass that covers the silent tomb of my friend.

The uncaring destruction of beings and all the misfortunes of humanity are counted as nothing in the grand scheme of things. The death of a kind man who expired in the quarters of his desolate friends and the death of a butterfly that the cool air of morning made perish in the chalice of a flower are two similar events in the course of nature. The man is only a phantom, a shadow, a vapor that dissipates in the air...

But the dawn begins to lighten the sky, the dark thoughts that bothered me vanish with the night, and hope is reborn in my heart. No, that which floods the east with light did not in the least make my gaze glisten only to plunge me so soon into the nothingness of night. The one who expanded this incomprehensible horizon, the one who lifts these enormous masses, for whom the sun gilds the frozen mountaintops, is also the one who ordered my heart to beat and my mind to think.

No, my friend did not enter into nothingness. Whatever the barrier that separates us may be, I will dream of him. It's not a syllogism that I found my hope. The flight of an insect through the air is enough to persuade me, and after the sight of the countryside, the perfume of the air and whatever charm is scattered about me thus lift my thoughts so that an unshakeable proof of immortality forcefully enters my soul and occupies it entirely.

Chapter 22

For a long time, the chapter that I just wrote would come to my pen, and I always rejected it. I had promised myself that I would only allow the laughing side of my soul to be seen, but I abandoned this project like so many others. I hope that the sensitive reader will pardon me for asking of him a few tears, and if someone feels that I actually could have omitted that chapter, he can rip it out of his copy or even throw the book in the fire.

It's enough for me that you find it in your heart, my dear Jenny—you, the best and most beloved of women; you, the best and most beloved of sisters—it's to you that I dedicate my work. If it has your approval, it would have that of all delicate and kind hearts. And if you pardon the madness that sometimes comes forth against my will, I will take on all the critics in the universe.

CHAPTER 23

I WILL ONLY SAY A word about the next print on the wall.

It's the family of the unfortunate Ugolino, made famous in Dante's *Inferno*, dying of hunger. One of his sons is stretched out motionless at his feet; the others hold their weakened arms out to him and ask for bread while the sad father is pressed up against prison bars, his eyes staring and distraught, his face immobile. In the horrible peace that gives the last period of despair, he dies both his own death and the deaths of his children, and suffers all that human nature can suffer.

Brave knight of Assas, there you are, dying by a hundred bayonets with a show of courage, a heroism that we can no longer recognize in our time!

And you who cry under these palms, sad Black woman! You who without a doubt were not from England, betrayed and neglected—what can I say? You who some man had the cruelty to sell like a vile slave in spite of your love and your service, despite the fruits of his attentions that you carry in your womb. I cannot pass before your image without paying you the homage that is due to your tenderness and to your misfortune!

Let's stop a minute before this next tableau: it's a young shepherdess who guards her flock all alone high in the Alps. She is seated on an old, fallen tree trunk bleached by many winters. Her feet are covered by the large leaves of a tuft of cacalia herbs, and lily flowers rise above her head. Lavender, thyme, anemone, star thistles, flowers of every species that are cultivated with care in our greenhouses and our gardens yet appear in the Alps in all their primitive beauty, form the bright carpet on which her sheep graze.

Friendly shepherdess, tell me where to find the happy corner of the earth where you live? From what distant cabin did you leave this morning at sunrise? Could I go live there with you?

But alas! The sweet tranquility that you enjoy will not delay its disappearance. The demon of war, not content to desolate cities, is soon going to bring trouble and fear to your solitary retreat. Already the soldiers advance; I see them climbing from mountain to mountain and approaching the clouds. The noise of the cannon can be heard in the high home of thunder. Flee, shepherdess; urge your herd on, hide yourself in the deepest and wildest caves. There is no more rest on this sad earth!

CHAPTER 24

I DON'T KNOW HOW IS happening. For some time, my chapters have been ending with a sinister tone. In vain, at the outset I fix my gaze on some nice object; in vain, I set out to be calm. I soon meet with a gust of wind that derails me. To put an end to this disturbance, which doesn't disrupt my thoughts, and to settle the racing of my heart, since so many calming images are too disturbing, I don't see any other remedy than an essay. Yes, I want to use it like ice over my heart.

This essay will be on painting, because there is not the least point in writing on any other subject. I can't descend fully from the point I was already climbing toward; besides, this is my hobby horse, like my uncle Toby had.

I would like to say, in passing, some words on the preeminence of the charming arts of painting and of music. Yes, I want to put something on the scales, if only a grain of sand, an atom.

They say in favor of the painter that he leaves something behind. His paintings survive him and extend the remembrance of him. Some respond that composers of music also leave operas and concerts, but music is subject to fashion, and painting isn't.

The bits of music that delighted our forefathers are absurd to the amateurs of our time. They place these works in comic operas, to make laugh the nephews of those whom they once made cry.

The paintings of Raphael enchant us in posterity as they amazed our ancestors.

This is my grain of sand.

Chapter 25

"BUT WHAT DOES IT MATTER to me," Madame de Hautcastel said to me one day, "that the music of Cherubini or Cimarosa differs from that of their predecessors? What does it matter to me that the old music makes me laugh, while the new deliciously affects me? Do my pleasures necessarily have to resemble those of my forebears in order for me to be happy? You speak to me of painting, an art that is only appreciated by a class with very few people in it, while music enchants all who breathe."

I don't know much, in this moment, that you could say to this observation, which is not how I expected to begin this chapter.

If I had foreseen it, maybe I wouldn't have undertaken this essay. And you shouldn't take this voyage at all for a tour given by a musician. I am not that at all, on my honor. No, I am not a musician; I swear to the heavens and all those who have heard me play violin.

But in supposing the artistic merit of both art and music is equal, it's not possible to force the conclusion of the merit of the art or the artist. You see children playing the harpsichord as grand masters; you never see a good twelve-year-old painter. The painter, besides taste and feeling, requires a thoughtful mind, which musicians can do without. Every day you see men without heads and hearts plucking a violin or a harp to their delight.

You can raise a human jackass to play the harpsichord, and when it is played by a true master, the soul can travel at its ease while the fingers mechanically pluck sounds with which the soul is not remotely involved.

If, meanwhile, someone argues that there is a distinction between music composition and execution, I admit I'm a bit embarrassed. Alas! If all the creators of essays were of good faith, this is how all essays would finish. In undertaking the examination of a question, you usually take a dogmatic tone because you decided your position in secret, as I did in favor of painting, though I professed a hypocritical impartiality. But the discussion itself raises the objection, and everything ends in doubt.

CHAPTER 26

NOW THAT I'M CALMER, I'M going to try to speak without emotion of the two portraits that follow the painting of the shepherdess in the Alps.

Raphael! Your portrait could have been painted by no one by you. What other would dare undertake it? Your open stance, sensitive and spiritual, broadcasts your character and your kindness.

To complement your shadow, I placed nearby the portrait of your mistress. Thanks to her, all the men of all the centuries will eternally ask how many sublime works the art world was deprived of by your premature death.

When I examine the portrait of Raphael, I feel almost overcome by a nearly religious respect for this great man who, in the bloom of his age, surpassed all antiquity, and whose paintings cause admiration and despair in modern artists. My soul, in admiring the portrait, suffers a movement of indignation at this Italian woman who preferred his love to his lover, and who extinguished in his breast this celestial flame, this divine genius.

Did you not know that sadly Raphael had announced a painting superior to *The Transfiguration*? Were you not aware that you held in your arms nature's favorite, the father of enthusiasm, a sublime genius, a god?

As my soul makes these observations, its companion, in fixing an attentive eye on the ravishing figure of this fateful beauty, feels ready to pardon her for the death of Raphael. In vain my soul reproaches the jackass for its extravagant weakness; it isn't listening at all. It places itself between these two ladies and, as happens on these kinds of occasions, strikes up a singular conversation that as usual ends in favoring bad principles, and from that I have taken a sample for another chapter.

CHAPTER 27

THE PRINTS AND THE PAINTINGS that I came over here to speak of pale and fade away at the first glimpse of the following painting. The immortal works of Raphael, of Corregio, and of all the Italians will not hold up in comparison. I always keep this one for last, as the ace up my sleeve, when I give a few curious people the pleasure of traveling with me. And I assure you that, whenever I had them view this painting—which is sublime to both connoisseurs and the ignorant, to people of the world, to artists, to women and children, even to animals—I have always seen the spectators give, each in their own way, some signs of pleasure and astonishment. Thus is nature admirably rendered there!

Ah! What painting could be presented to you,

gentlemen; what spectacle could be set before your eyes, ladies, that could be more sure of your approval than the faithful representation of yourself? The painting I speak of is a mirror. No one so far has yet wanted to critique it. It is, for all who look at it, a perfect painting about which there is nothing to say.

You would think without a doubt that it should be counted as one of the marvels of this country where I travel.

I will pass in silence with the pleasure that comes over the natural philosopher on the strange phenomena of the light as it represents all the objects of nature on its smooth surface.

The mirror presents to the sedentary voyager a thousand interesting reflections, a thousand observations that render it a useful and precious object.

You, whom Love held or still holds under its rule, learn that being in front of a mirror is what sharpens its traits and contemplates its cruelties. It's there that it practices its maneuvers, that it prepares for the advance to the war it wants to declare; it's there that it practices its sweet gazes and little expressions, the knowing sulks, like an actor practices his expressions before appearing in public. Always impartial and true, a mirror reflects to the eyes of the spectator the roses of youth and the wrinkles of age without slander and without flattery. Alone among the councilors of great men, it consistently tells them the truth.

This advantage made me wish for the invention of a moral mirror, where all men could see themselves along with their vices and virtues. I considered even offering a fee to some academy for this discovery when I realized the full reflection would be unusable.

Alas! It is so rare that the ugly person recognizes themselves and smashes the mirror. In vain, the glass multiplies around us and reflects with geometric precision the light and the truth. At the moment where the rays penetrate our eye and depict us such as we are, narcissism slides its deceitful prism between us and our image and presents us as a divinity. And of all the prisms that have existed since the first to leave the hand of the immortal Newton, none have possessed a force of refraction so powerful and produced colors so lovely and vivid as the prism of narcissism.

Well, since common mirrors tell the truth in vain, and since each is content with what he sees, and you can't make men recognize their physical imperfections, what good would my moral mirror do? Few in the world would glance at it, and no one would recognize themselves—except the philosophers. I even doubt they would, a little.

In taking the mirror for what it is, I hope that no one blames me for having placed it above all the paintings from the Italians. Women, for whom taste would not be false and whose decisions should rule all, usually glance first on this painting when they enter an apartment.

I have seen a thousand times ladies, and even young men, forget their lovers or mistresses, the dance, and all the pleasures of a ball to contemplate, with a marked ease, this enchanting painting and honor it from time to time with a glance in the middle of an animated dance.

Who could then argue with the rank I accord this masterwork among the art of Apelles?

Chapter 28

I HAD FINALLY ARRIVED AT my desk. Even so, if I extended my arms, I could have touched the corner nearest to me. That's when I saw myself on the verge of witnessing the destruction of the fruits of all my work and losing my life. I should pass by the accident that happened to me in silence so as not to discourage other travelers, but it is so difficult to turn over the post-chaise, a small two-wheeled carriage that I use, that you would have to admit that it was very unlucky. It was also unlucky that I was in it and courting such a danger.

I found myself laid out on the ground so quickly and unexpectedly that I would have been tempted to doubt my unluckiness if a ringing in my head and a stabbing pain in my left shoulder didn't provide more than enough evidence of its truth.

This was yet another trick by my jackass.

Frightened by the voice of a beggar who suddenly asked for alms at my door, plus the barking of Rosine, "the other" turned brusquely in my post-chaise before my soul had time to realize that the brick that served as a drag was gone. The jackass's jerk was so violent that my post-chaise was thrown from its center of gravity, and it fell over on top of me.

Here is, I admit, one of the occasions where I had to pity my soul the most. Instead of being angered by its absence in the affair and berating its companion for its fall, it forgot itself and shared the most bestial resentment and began berating the poor man.

"Lazy bum! Get a job!" it yelled at him. (A horrid insult invented by the greedy, cruel rich!)

"Sir," he said by way of explanation, "I'm from Chambéry..."

"Too bad for you."

"I'm Jacques; you saw me in the country. I herded the sheep in the fields."

"What do you do here?" My soul began to repent of the brutality of my first few words. I even think that it had repented in the instant before letting them fly. It's like when you see a ditch or a slough as you're walking but you don't make any attempt to avoid it.

Rosine managed to bring me back to my senses and say she was sorry. She had recognized Jacques, who had shared his bread with her. He now proved he remembered her too and recognized her by petting her.

All this time, Joannetti, having gathered his share of my dinner for himself, gave it without hesitating to Jacques. Poor Joannetti!

Thus in my travels I am going to take lessons in philosophy and humanity from my butler and my dog.

CHAPTER 29

BEFORE GOING ANY FARTHER, I'M going to squash a doubt that could be introduced in the minds of my readers.

I would not want for all the world to be suspected of having solely undertaken this voyage only because I was forced, in some manner, by circumstances. I assure you here and swear by all that is dear that I had planned this undertaking long before the event that caused me to lose my liberty for forty-two days. This forced retreat was only an occasion for setting out on my route sooner.

I know that the free protestation that I make here will seem suspect to certain people, but I also know that suspicious people won't read this book. They're already preoccupied with their own households and friends; they have enough other affairs. And good people will believe me.

I admit that I would have preferred to make this voyage another time and that I would have chosen to execute it during the Lenten fast instead of Carnival. However, philosophical reflections that come to me from heaven have greatly helped to buoy me through the deprivation of pleasures that Turin presents in this loud, crowded time. It is certain, I have thought, that the walls of my room are not as magnificently decorated as those of a ballroom; the silence of my surroundings doesn't compare to the happy sound of music and dancing. But among the brilliant personalities that you meet at these parties are those who are certainly more boring than me. And why would I fixate on considering those who are in a more pleasant situation than mine while the world teems with more unfortunate people? Instead of transporting myself via imagination in this superb apartment, where such beauties are eclipsed by the young Eugenie, to find myself happy, I only have to stop for an instant along the streets where the revelers drive. A heap of wretches nestled half-naked under the porticos of these sumptuous apartments seem near to dying of cold and misery.

What a sight! I wish that this page of my book was known to the whole universe. I wish it was known that in this city, where everyone breathes opulence, during the coldest nights of winter a crowd of miserable wretches sleeps in the open, heads resting on a curb or on the threshold of a palace.

Here is a group of children clutching one another so as not to die of cold. There is a shivering woman without a voice to complain. Passersby come and go without being moved by a sight they've grown accustomed to. The noise of coaches, the voices of intemperance, and the ravishing sounds of music mingle at times with the cries of the unfortunate to create a horrible dissonance.

Chapter 30

THOSE WHO RUSH TO JUDGE a town after the preceding chapter are very much fooling themselves. I spoke of the poor who are found there, of their pitiable cries, and of the indifference of some people to their plight. But I said nothing of the crowd of charitable men who sleep while others amuse themselves, who get up at the crack of dawn and go help the wretches without witness or ostentation.

No, I will not pass by them without note. I want to write on these pages what everyone should read.

Having so shared their fortune with their brothers, after having poured a balm onto these hearts crumpled by sadness, they go into the churches, while tired vice sleeps on the mattress, to offer to

God their prayers and thanks for their benefactors. The light of the solitary lamp inside the temple still struggles against that of the breaking day, and already they have bowed at the feet of the altar. The Eternal, irritated by the hardness and the avarice of men, draws back his lightning bolt, ready to strike.

CHAPTER 31

I WANTED TO SAY SOMETHING about the unfortunates in my travels because the idea of their misery often came to distract me on my path. Sometimes struck by the difference between their situation and mine, I would suddenly stop my progress, and my room would seem to be extravagantly embellished. What useless luxury! Six chairs! Two tables! A desk! A mirror! What ostentation! My bed—above all my bed, in rose and white—and my two mattresses seemed to me to rival the magnificence and the softness of Asian royalty.

These reflections rendered me indifferent to the pleasures they forbid my attending. Reflecting on reflections, my philosophical mood became such that I heard a ball in the neighboring apartment, or heard the sound of violins or clarinets, without stirring from my spot. I heard with my own two ears the melodious voice of Marchesini, this voice that so had often taken me away from myself; yes, I heard it without moving. Moreover, I regarded without the least emotion the most beautiful woman in Turin, Eugenie herself, adorned from head to toe by the hands of Mademoiselle Repous. That is, however, not as certain.

CHAPTER 32

Bᴜᴛ ᴀʟʟᴏᴡ ᴍᴇ ᴛᴏ ᴀsᴋ you, sirs: do you still enjoy yourselves at balls and at the theater as much as you did in the old days? For myself, I confess that for some time all the many gatherings have inspired in me a kind of terror. There I am beset by a sinister vision. In vain I attempt to chase it away, but it always comes back, like that of Racine's *Athalie*. Maybe it's because my soul, inundated these days with dark visions and heartbreaking scenes, finds sad subjects everywhere, like a bad stomach that converts to poison the healthiest of foods.

Whatever it may be, here is my vision: when I'm at one of these parties, in the middle of this crowd of amiable and affectionate men who dance, who sing, who cry at tragedies, who only express cheer, candor, and cordiality, I say to myself, What if, in this polite assembly, all of a sudden a polar bear enters— or a philosopher, a tiger, or some other animal of this kind—and goes up to the orchestra and cries in a frenzied voice, "Unfortunate humans! Listen to the truth that is coming from my mouth: you are oppressed, tyrannized; you are wretches; you bore yourselves. Leave this lethargy!

"You, musicians, begin by smashing these instruments over your heads, and arm yourselves with a dagger. Don't think any more of the future of vacations or parties. Climb to the lodge and cut everyone's throat. Let the women also soak their timid hands in blood!

"Go, you are free. Pull your king down from his throne and your God from his sanctuary!"

Well! How many of these charming men will execute what the tiger said? How many maybe thought about doing it before the tiger even asked? Who knows? Weren't they dancing in Paris five years ago?

"Joannetti, close the doors and windows. I don't want to see the light. Let no man enter my room; put my saber by the door where I can grab it; leave and never darken my doorstep again!"

Chapter 33

" No, no, stay, Joannetti. Stay, poor boy. And you too, my Rosine, you who predict my pain and who lessen it with your affections. Come, my Rosine, come. Letter V and stay."

CHAPTER 34

THE FALL OF MY LITTLE post-chaise renders the service to the reader of cutting short my voyage by a good dozen chapters, because in bringing it up I found myself face-to-face with my desk. I no longer had time to reflect on a number of prints and paintings that I had yet to get around to. That could have extended my digression on painting.

I'm rightly leaving behind, then, the portraits of Raphael and his mistress, the knight Assas and the shepherdess in the Alps. On the left side of the window, we discover my desk. It's the first and most obvious thing that presents itself to the gaze of the traveler following the route that I have set out.

Above it are some shelves serving as a library, crowned by a bust that finishes the pyramid. This is the object that contributes the most decoration to the land.

In opening the first drawer on the right, we find writing supplies—paper of all kinds, pens of all sizes, wax to close the letters. All this would cause even the most indolent to want to write. I am sure, my dear Jenny, that if you came to open this drawer by accident, you would answer the letter that I wrote you last year. In the corresponding drawer lie confusing piles of materials for the moving story of the prisoner of Pignerol, which you will read soon, my dear friends. Between these two drawers is a nook where I stack the letters so I can measure how many I've received. You'll find there all the letters I've received over ten years. The oldest are arranged by date in several bundles; the newest are random; the remaining letters date from my childhood.

What a pleasure it is to see in these letters the interesting situations of our younger years, to be transported anew to those happy times that we'll never see again!

Ah! My heart is so full and bittersweet as my eyes travel along the lines written out by a being who no longer exists. Here are his characters; it is his heart that drives his hand. It's to me that he wrote this letter, and this letter is all of him that remains with me.

Whenever I hold this reduction of him in my hand, it is rare that I can pull through the rest of the day. It's like the voyager who crosses rapidly some

Italian province, in his haste making some superficial observations, to take up residence in Rome for the entire month. It's the richest vein of the mine that I exploit.

What changes in my thoughts and feelings! What changes in my friends! When I examine them then and today, I seem them as being disturbed nearly to death by plans that don't affect them at all now. We watched some event as a great misfortune, but the end of the letter is missing, and the event is completely forgotten. I can't know what he was asking.

A thousand prejudices besiege us; the world and men are totally unknown to us, but also there's such warmth in our trade. What intimate meetings! What confidants without borders!

We were glad for our mistakes. And now, ah! That's no longer so. We had to read, like the others, into the human heart. And that truth, falling amongst us like a bomb, destroyed forever the enchanted palace of illusion.

CHAPTER 35

I T WOULD ONLY BE WORTH it to me to do a chapter on this dried rose if the subject is worth the trouble. It's a Carnival flower from last year. I myself went to pick it in Valentine's greenhouse, and that evening, an hour before the ball, full of hope and in a good mood, I went to give it to Madame de Hautcastel. She took it and put it down on her vanity without looking at it—or even at me.

But how could she pay attention to me? She was occupied with regarding herself. Standing in front of a tall mirror, her hair done up, she placed a hand on her dress. She was so very much occupied, her attention so totally absorbed by her ribbons, gauze, and pompoms of all sorts piled up on her costume, that I couldn't get even a glance from her, a sign. I resigned myself. I humbly held some pins arranged at the ready in my hand. But her pincushion being more within reach, she took them from there. If I advanced my hand, she took the pins from my hand indifferently, groping around without taking her eyes from the mirror for fear of losing the view.

For some time I held a second mirror behind her so she could better judge her costume, and, with her figure repeating from one mirror to the other, I then saw a perspective of coquettes. Not one of them would pay attention to me. Really, what could I say to her? We made, my rose and I, a very sad pair.

I ended up losing my patience, and not being able to resist the fit of pique that came over me, I set in front of the mirror what I was holding in my hand, and I left angrily and without taking her leave.

"Are you going?" she asked me while turning sideways to see her profile. I didn't answer, but I listened for some time at the door to learn what effect my abrupt departure was going to produce. "Don't you see," she said to her maid after a moment of silence, "don't you see that this caraco is much too large for me, especially on the bottom, and that it will have to be pinned up?"

How and why this dried rose finds itself there on a shelf of my desk, that's what I won't go into, because I declared already that a dried rose wouldn't merit a chapter.

Note well, ladies, that I didn't reflect at all on the adventure of the dried rose. I only said that Madame de Hautcastel had, for better or for worse, preferred her dress to me, not that I had any right to be received otherwise by her.

I take much care in not taking too much from this story about the general consequences of reality or the strength and duration of the affection of women for their friends. I'm happy to throw this chapter—since it is one now—to throw it, I say, into the world along with the rest of the voyage without addressing it to anyone and without recommending it to anyone.

I'll only add a bit of advice for you, gentlemen: bear in mind that on a ball day, your mistress is no longer yours. At the moment when dressing begins, the lover is no longer a husband, and the ball alone becomes the lover.

Everyone knows, moreover, what few gains a husband can make by forcing his love. Take your hurt with patience and laughter.

And don't suffer any illusions, sir. If you're regarded with pleasure at the ball, it's not at all because of your quality as a lover or because you are her husband. It's because you are part of the ball and are consequently a fraction of her new conquest. You are a decimal of a lover. Maybe it's because you dance well and you help her shine. After all, it's probably more flattering for you to be received well by her. She hopes that in declaring as her lover a man of merit like yourself, she will fan the flames of jealousy in her companions. Without this consideration, she would not have looked only at you.

Here then is what I've heard. You must resign yourself and wait for your role of husband to arise. I know those who would like to be let go at such a bargain rate.

Chapter 36

I HAD PROMISED A DIALOGUE between my soul and "the other," but certain chapters keep coming forth; rather, other chapters flow from my pen in spite of my intentions and derail my projects. This chapter is about my library, which I will make as short as possible. The forty-two days are going to end, and an equal amount of time will not be sufficient to create the rich description of this country where I travel happily.

I must confess, my library is composed of novels. Yes, novels, and some poetry too.

As if I didn't have enough problems, I still voluntarily divide up these thousand imaginary people, and I deeply feel for them as if they were my own. Didn't I shed tears for the unlucky Clarissa Harlowe and the lover of Charlotte in *Werther*?

But though I look for such faint afflictions, I find on the other hand in this imaginary world virtue, kindness, and altruism as I've not yet found in the real world where I live. I find there a woman as I desire her, without whims, without lightness, without subterfuge. I say nothing of beauty. You can trust my imagination—I make her so beautiful that there is nothing left to say.

Finally closing the book, which no longer holds my interest, I take her by the hand, and we head off together across a country a thousand times more wonderful than Eden. What painter could represent the enchanted countryside where I have placed the divinity of my heart? And what poet could ever describe the vivid and varied sensations that I feel in these enchanted lands?

How many times have I not cursed this *Cleveland*, who sets out on a whim for new misfortunes that he could have avoided! I cannot suffer this book and this chain of calamities, but if I open it without thinking, I have to read it through to the end. How can I leave this poor man among the Abaquis? What will become of him with those savages? I dare even less to abandon him during the excursion that he takes to escape his captivity.

At last, I enter so far into his troubles, I take such a strong interest in him and his ill-fated family that the unexpected arrival of the ghost of ferocious Ruintons stands my hair on end. A cold sweat covers me when I read this passage, and my fright is so vivid, so real, as if I should be roasted myself and eaten by this crook.

When I've cried enough and made love, I look for something poetic, and I leave anew for another world.

CHAPTER 37

FROM THE ADVENTURE OF THE Argonauts to the Assembly of Notables convened by the king, from the depths of Hell to the last star in the Milky Way to the edges of the universe to the doors of chaos, here is the vast field where I walk far and wide, and all at my leisure. Neither time nor space matter to me. This is where I transport my very existence to the place of Homer, Milton, Virgil, Ossian, etc.

All events that take place between these two poles, all the countries, all the worlds, and all the beings that have existed between these two terminals, all this to me seems so good, as legitimate as the ships that follow in Piraeus belonging to a certain Athenian.

I love above all the poets who bring me into the highest antiquity: the death of the ambitious

Agamemnon, the rages of Orestes, and the whole tragic story of the family of Atreus persecuted by heaven. They inspire in me a terror that modern events do not.

Here is the urn that contains the ashes of Orestes. Who wouldn't shudder at the sight? Electra! Sad sister, calm yourself. It's Orestes himself who brings the urn, and the ashes are those of his enemies.

We no longer regard the shores as those of Xanthus or Scamander. We no longer see the plains as those of Hesperides or of Arcadia. Where today are the isles of Lemnos and Crete? Where is the famous labyrinth? Where is the rock that the abandoned Ariadne soaked with tears? We no longer see Theseus and still less of Hercules. The men and even the heroes of today are stunted.

When I want to treat myself to an enthusiastic scene and play with all the forces of my imagination, I place myself firmly in the folds of the floating gown of the sublime blind poet Albion at the moment where he hurls himself into the sky and dares approach the eternal throne. What muse was able to support this hauteur, where no man before him had dared to raise his gaze? From the dazzling celestial facade that the miserly Mammon would look at with his greedy gaze, I pass with horror into the vast caverns of Satan's dwelling. I assist in infernal counsel, I melt into a crowd of rebel spirits, and I listen to their discussions.

But I have to own up to a weakness that I often

reproach myself for.

I can't help taking a certain interest in poor Satan (I am speaking specifically of Milton's Satan) since he fell from heaven. Everyone blames the obstinacy of the rebel spirit, but I say that the steadfastness that he shows in his excess of misfortune and the greatness of his courage force me to admire him despite myself.

But I don't disregard the evils derived from the deadly enterprise that drove him to force open the doors of Hell to come harass our original parents. But I cannot, whatever I do, wish for a moment to see him perish on a path of confusion and chaos. I even believe that I would choose to help him without any shame holding me back. I follow all his movements, and I find such pleasure in traveling with him as if I were in good company. I know full well that, after all, he's the devil and that this is a path for losing humankind, that this is a true democracy, not like those in Athens but like those of Paris. All those could not cure me of my opinion.

What a vast project! And what daring in its execution!

When the gigantic threefold gates of Hell opened suddenly before him, and as the deep grave of nothingness and night appeared at his feet in all its horror, he ran an unwavering eye over the somber empire of chaos. Opening his massive wings, which could cloak an entire army, he dropped into the abyss.

I call him one of the boldest. And that, according

to me, is one of the best uses of imagination for one of the best voyages that has ever been made—after the voyage around my room.

CHAPTER 38

I WOULDN'T FINISH IF I described even the thousandth part of the singular events that come to me when I travel near my library. The voyages of Cook and the observations of his traveling companions, Doctors Banks and Solander, are nothing in comparison to my adventures in this district alone. Also, I think that I would have passed my life there in a state of ecstasy without the bust of which I spoke, upon which my eyes and my thoughts always end up fixating. Such is the situation of my soul, and when it is too violently stirred, or it has been given over to discouragement, I have only to look at this bust to put it back in its natural place. It's the tuning fork I use to align the variable and discordant assemblage of sensations and perceptions that form my existence.

How lifelike the bust is! See here the traits that nature had given to this most virtuous of men. Ah! If the sculptor could only have rendered visible his excellent soul, his genius and character! But do I dare undertake this? Is this, then, the place to deliver his elegy? Is it to the people who tour with me that I address it? Eh, what do they care either way?

I am happy to prostrate myself in front of your cherished image, oh, the best of fathers! Alas! This image is all that remains with me of you and of my inherited lands. You left this earth at the moment when crime was about to overrun it. Such are the evils that overwhelmed us that your family is now forced to regard your loss as a blessing. What evils you had to suffer over your long life! O my father, does your large family know of you in the place of happiness? Do you know that your children were exiled from their homeland, which you had served for sixty years with such zeal and integrity? Do you know that the family is prevented from visiting your tomb? But the tyranny could not erase for them the most precious part of your legacy: the memory of your virtue and the strength of your example. In the midst of the criminal flood that follows their patriarch and their fortune into the abyss, they have remained stead-fastly on the line that you drew for them. And when they can again bow down on your venerated ashes, you will again recognize them.

CHAPTER 39

I PROMISED A DIALOGUE, AND I'm keeping my
word. It was morning at the dawn of the day: the
rays of the sun gilded the summit of Mont Viso
and the tallest mountains of the island at our antip-
odes. Already the jackass was risen; maybe its premature awakening was the effect of the night visions that
often put it in a state of agitation as tiring as it is
useless, or maybe it was the Carnival, which was then
nearing its end, that was the occult cause of its awakening. This time of pleasure and folly has an influe-
ence on the human machine much like the phases of
the moon and the conjunction of certain planets. In
the end, it was roused and very wide awake when my
soul lifted itself from drowsiness.

For quite a while, my confused soul shared the

sensations of "the other," but it was still wrapped in the black ribbons of night and sleepiness. These ribbons seemed to transform into gauze, into linen, into cloth of India. My poor soul was then wrapped up in all this paraphernalia, and the god of sleep, to keep my soul firmly within his empire, added to its bonds tousled blond tresses, knotted ribbons, and pearl necklaces. Anyone who would have seen it struggling in these wisps would have pitied it.

The agitation of the most noble part of myself spoke to "the other," and the latter in its turn worked powerfully on my soul. I was reaching a state difficult to describe when at last my soul, maybe through wisdom, maybe by accident, found the way to free itself from the gauze that suffocated it. I don't know if it happened on an opening or if it simply lifted them out of the way, which is more natural. The fact is that it found an exit from the labyrinth.

The locks of tangled hair were still there, but they were no longer an obstacle; they were rather average. My soul seized them like a drowning man clings to the grass on the riverbank. But the pearl necklace broke in the struggle, and the pearls came unstrung. They rolled onto the sofa and then onto the parquet floor of Madame de Hautcastel because my soul, by a bizarre chance that would be difficult to reasonably explain, imagined itself being at this woman's house.

A fat bouquet of violets fell to the ground, and my soul woke up then, went home, and brought reason and reality to the scene. As you would imagine, it strongly disapproved of all that had happened in its absence, and this is where we begin the dialogue that is the subject of this chapter.

My soul had never been so poorly received. The reproaches that it thought appropriate to make in this critical moment managed to stir up strife. This was a revolt, a formal insurrection.

"What now?" said my soul. "I see that, during my absence, instead of preparing your forces for a quiet awakening and properly returning to execute my orders, you insolently decided (the term being a little strong) to give yourself over to the transports that my will did not sanction?"

Not being accustomed to this haughty tone, "the other" answered angrily, "It suits you well, madame (to underline in the discussion the whole idea of familiarity), it suits you well to give yourself airs of decadence and of virtue. Isn't it due to the gaps in your imagination and your extravagant ideals that I must be all that you dislike? Why weren't you there? Why do you have the right to enjoy things without me in the frequent voyages that you make all alone? I have never disapproved of your meetings in the heavens or in the Elysian Fields, your conversations with the intelligentsia, your deep speculations (a little taunt, you see), your castles in Spain, your sublime systems? And don't I have the right when you leave me behind to enjoy the kindnesses that are given to me by nature and the pleasures that it presents to me?"

My soul, very surprised at this liveliness and elo-
quence, didn't know how to answer.

To settle the matter, it began to cover the
reproaches with a veil of benevolence as much as it
could allow and, in order to not seem to be taking
the first step toward reconciliation, it imagined putting on a ceremonial tone.

"Madame," it said in its turn with an affected
cordiality (if the reader found this word out of place
when addressing my soul, what will he say now when
recalling the subject of this dispute? My soul doesn't
feel insulted at all by this manner of speaking. So
much does passion dim intelligence!) "Madame,"
it said, "I assure you that nothing would give me as
much pleasure as seeing you enjoy all the pleasures to
which our nature is susceptible, even if I don't share
them, as long as these pleasures weren't harmful to
you and if they didn't alter the harmony that—"

Here my soul was rudely interrupted. "No, no,
I am not duped by your supposed benevolence. The
enforced stay that we're enduring together in this
room where we travel, the wound that I received that
very nearly destroyed me and that still bleeds—isn't
all this the fruit of your extravagant pride and your
barbaric prejudices? My well-being and even my
existence count as nothing to you when your passions are roused. You pretend that you're interested
in me and that your insults come from friendship."

My soul saw clearly that it hadn't played the best
role on this occasion. It began to see that the heat of

the argument had overtaken its cause, and it used the circumstances to make a diversion.

"Make coffee," it said to Joannetti, who had entered the room. The noise of cups attracted all the attention of the insurgent, and in an instant it forgot all the rest. It's like showing a rattle to a toddler; it makes them forget the unhealthy snacks they demand while stamping their feet.

I dozed while the water heated.

I enjoyed this charming pleasure, which I have already shared with my readers, that you feel when you're sleepy. The agreeable noise made by Joannetti in tapping the coffee pot against the china rang in my skull and vibrated my sensitive nerves like plucking a harp string to make the octaves resonate. At last I saw a shadow in front of me. I opened my eyes. It was Joannetti. Ah! What perfume! What a nice surprise! Coffee! With cream! A stack of toast! Good reader, lunch with me.

Chapter 40

What a treasure trove of pleasures benevolent nature gives to men whose hearts know joy! And what a variety of pleasures! Who could count their innumerable nuances in diverse individuals and in different ages of life? The confused memory of my childhood pleasures still makes me tremble. Will I try to paint the suffering young man in whom the heart is beginning to burn with all the fires of feeling at this happy age where we still don't know the names of interest, of ambition, of hate, and of all the shameful passions that degrade and torment humanity? At this age, which is alas too short, the sun shines brightly in a way we won't see again for the rest of our lives. The air is more pure, the fountains run more clear and fresh, nature has aspects and the groves have paths that we won't find again when we are mature. God! What perfumes emanate from the flowers! What delicious fruits! What colors adorn the dawn! All women are friendly and faithful; all men are good, generous, and wise. Above all we meet with cordiality, candor, and generosity. Only flowers, virtues, and pleasures exist in nature.

The emotion of love, the hope of happiness—don't they flood our hearts with feelings both vivid and various?

The spectacle of nature and its contemplation as a whole and in detail opens an immense pit of pleasures before our reason. Soon the imagination, in surfing this ocean of pleasures, grows in number and intensity. Diverse sensations unite and combine to form something new. Dreams of glory meld with palpitations of love. Charity walks by the side of self-esteem, which takes its hand. Melancholy comes from time to time to throw its solemn veil over us and change our tears to pleasures. At last, the perceptions of the mind, the sensations of the heart, and even the memories of meaning are for mankind inexhaustible sources of pleasure and happiness. It's not surprising at all that the noise that Joannetti makes in tapping the coffeepot against the china and the unexpected appearance of a cup of cream leaves an impression so vivid and agreeable.

CHAPTER 41

I IMMEDIATELY PUT ON MY traveling clothes after having examined them with an eye toward convenience, and that's when I decided to do an ad hoc chapter to explain this to the reader. The form and utility of traveling clothes being generally well enough known, I will describe particularly their influence on the mind of the traveler.

My traveling garb for winter is made of the warmest, wooliest stuff that I could find. It wraps me entirely from head to toe, and when I am in my chair, hands in my pockets and head pulled inside my collar, I resemble the statue of Vishnu without feet or hands, like you see in Indian pagodas.

One could accuse me, if one wanted, of predetermining the influence on travelers that I attribute to travel clothing. All I can say for certain to this consideration is that it appears to me as silly to take a single step in my voyage around my room decked out in my uniform with sword at my side as it would be to leave here and go out into the world in my bathrobe. When I see myself so dressed, following all the pragmatic rigors, not only am I not even able to continue my voyage but I believe that I wouldn't even be in a state to read what I've just written, let alone understand it.

Does this astonish you? Don't we see people every day who believe they're sick because their beard is too long, or because someone else thinks they look sick and says so to them? Clothing has this same sort of influence on the spirit of men as it does on those of fragile health who find themselves feeling much better when they see themselves in new outfits and powdered wigs. They see that it fools the public as well as themselves to dress up. Then they die on a beautiful morning, all done up, and their death shocks everyone.

Sometimes they forgot to warn the Comte de ——— several days in advance before it was his turn to guard. A corporal went to wake him at a very early hour the day the comte had to mount up and announced the bad news. But the idea of suddenly getting up, putting on his gaiters, and going out without having planned for it the day before troubled him so much that he preferred to say he was sick and not leave his house. He then put on his dressing gown and dismissed the barber. This gave him a pale, sickly countenance that alarmed his wife and family. He really found himself a little defeated that day.

He told everyone he was sick—a little to support his bet, and a little because he believed himself to be ill. The influence of the dressing gown began to work. The broth that he took, willing patient that he was, nauseated him. Soon his parents and friends sent to ask for news. It was enough to send him to bed for real.

That evening, Dr. Ranson found his pulse to be elevated and ordered him to be bled the next day. If the campaign had lasted a month longer, he would have been beyond illness.

Who could doubt the influence of traveling clothes on travelers when they reflect that the poor Comte de —— thought it he was about to make the trip to the other world for having put on his robe in bad faith in this one?

CHAPTER 42

I WAS SITTING NEAR MY fire after dinner, nestled inside my traveling clothes and giving myself over to their influence while waiting for the hour of departure, when the haze of indigestion came over my mind and so obstructed the paths my ideas travel along when coming to my consciousness that all communication was intercepted. My consciousness no longer transmitted any ideas to my brain, and my brain in turn could no longer carry the electric fluid that animates my ideas and resuscitates the dead frogs of the ingenious Dr. Valli.

You can easily imagine, after having read this preamble, why my head fell to my chest and how the muscles of my thumb and index finger of my right hand, being no longer energized by this fluid, relaxed to the point that a volume of the works of Caraccioli that I held tightly between these two digits escaped my grasp without my noticing and fell to the hearth.

I had just received visitors, and my conversation with the people who had left had centered on the recent death of the famous Dr. Cigna, who was universally mourned. He was smart, hardworking, a good physician, and a famed botanist. The merit of this skillful man occupied my thoughts; however, I said to myself, if he allowed me to call upon the souls of all those whom he may have ushered into the next world, who knows if his reputation would suffer a knock?

I was unwittingly headed for a dissertation on medicine and the progress it had made since Hippocrates. I asked myself if the famous people of antiquity who died in their beds, like Aspasia and Hippocrates himself, had died like ordinary people, with a putrid fever, inflammatory and verminous, and if they had been bled and crammed with remedies.

I can't say why I reflected on these four personages instead of others. Who can render reason from a dream? All I can say is that it was my soul that brought forth the doctor from Cos, the doctor from Turin, and the famous man of state who made such beautiful things and committed such massive faults.

As for his elegant friend, I humbly avow that it was "the other" that motioned toward her. However, when I think of it, I would be tempted to feel a little bit of pride. It is clear that, on reflection, the balance in favor of reason was four to one. That's a lot for a military man of my age.

Whatever it may be, while I gave myself over to these reflections, my eyes allowed themselves to close, and I slept deeply. In closing my eyes, the image of those personages whom I had thought remained painted on this fine film we call memory mingled in my brain with the idea of calling up the dead. I soon saw Hippocrates, Plato, Pericles, Aspasia, and Dr. Cigna with his wig arriving.

I saw them all sit down on the chairs still arrayed by the fire. Pericles alone remained standing to read the newspapers.

"If these discoveries that you tell me about are true," said the doctor Hippocrates, "and if they have been as useful to medicine as you say, I would have seen the number of men who descend into the somber kingdom diminish. And that ratio, according to the registers of Minos, which I have verified myself, is constantly the same."

Dr. Cigna turned toward me. "You have doubtless heard tell of these discoveries?" he said to me. "You're aware of this Harvey on the circulation of the blood, this immortal Spallanzani on digestion, so that we now know all its mechanics?" He went on to give a long list of all the discoveries in medicine and of the remedies that were due to chemistry. It was an academic discourse in favor of modern medicine.

"Am I to believe," I said, "that these great men

are unaware of all that you just said to them, and that their souls, freed from the hindrances of the material world, find anything obscure in all of nature?"

"Ah! That is your error!" cried the proto-doctor from the Peloponnesus. "The mysteries of natures are hidden for the dead as for the living. He who created and who directs all, he alone knows the great secret that men await in vain. Here is what we learn for certain on the banks of the Styx—and believe me," he added, addressing his words to Hippocrates, "strip yourself of the esprit de corps that you've brought to the place of mortals. Since the work of a thousand generations and all the discoveries of men has not lengthened their existence a single instant, while Charon passes in his boat each day the same number of shades, we will not tire in defending an art that, in the house of death, won't even be useful to doctors." Thus spoke the famed Hippocrates, to my great astonishment.

Dr. Cigna laughed. As spirits cannot refuse evidence nor be silent regarding the truth, not only did he share the opinion of Hippocrates, but he even professed, while blushing in the manner of intellectuals, that he had always suspected this.

Pericles, approaching from the window, let out a great sigh, and I could guess its cause. He read an issue of the *Monitor* that announced the decadence of the arts and sciences; he saw illustrious wise men leave their sublime speculations to invent new crimes; and he shuddered on hearing a horde of cannibals being compared to the heroes of generous Greece for killing on the scaffold, without shame or remorse, venerable old men, women, and children and committing in cold blood the most atrocious and useless crimes.

Plato, who had listened to our conversation without saying anything and now saw it suddenly end in an unexpected manner, took his turn to speak.

"I see," he said to us, "how the discoveries that were made by your great men in all the branches of physics are not useful to medicine, which can never change the course of nature at the cost of the lives of men. But it will not be the same undoubtedly for the research that's being done on politics. The discoveries of Locke on the nature of the human mind, the invention of printing, the accumulated observations extracted from history...such profound books that have spread science to the people; such marvels have without doubt contributed to making men better. This happy and wise republic that I have imagined, and that the century in which I lived seemed to regard as an impractical dream, surely exists in the world today?"

To this question, the honest doctor lowered his eyes and only answered with tears. Then, as he wiped them with his handkerchief, he accidentally spun his wig so that part of his face was hidden.

"Immortal gods!" said Aspasia in a piercing cry. "What a strange figure! Is it then a discovery of your great men that you should coif yourselves with the scalp of another?"

Aspasia, who yawned at philosophical dissertations, had snatched up a fashion magazine that was on the fireplace. She had been leafing through it for some time when the doctor's wig had made him cry out. As the narrow, wobbly bench on which she was seated was quite uncomfortable for her, she placed her bare legs, decorated with wrappings, on the straw chair between her and I and pressed an elbow on Plato's wide shoulders.

"It's not a scalp at all," answered the doctor, taking his wig and throwing it into the fire. "It's a wig, mademoiselle, and I don't know why I didn't throw this ridiculous bit of frippery into the flames of Tartarus when I first got here. But idiocies and prejudice are so inherent in our miserable nature that they sometimes follow us all the way to the grave."

I took a singular pleasure in seeing the doctor renounce his medicine and his wig.

"I assure you," Aspasia said to him, "that most of the hairstyles shown in the magazine that I leaf through merit the same treatment as yours. They are so extravagant!"

The lovely Athenian was extremely amused by running her eye over those images and astonished at the variety and the oddity of modern tailoring. One model among the others struck her: a young lady shown with a most elegant coiffure, which Aspasia found a little too tall. But the length of gauze that circled her throat was of a fullness so extraordinary that you had to make an effort to see half her face. Aspasia, not knowing that these prodigious forms were merely due to starch, couldn't keep herself from showing an astonishment that would have been double (in the opposite direction) if the gauze had been transparent.

"But do explain to us," she said, "why women today seem to have clothes to hide themselves instead of to dress themselves? They barely let their faces be seen, though it's the only way to recognize their sex, as the shape of their bodies is disfigured by the bizarre pleats of fluff! Of all the figures that are shown in this magazine, none leave their throat, their arms, their legs uncovered. How are your young warriors not tempted to destroy a costume like this? Apparently," she added, "the virtue of women today, which is apparent in all their clothing, surpasses by far that of my contemporaries."

In finishing these words, Aspasia looked at me and seemed to require a response. I pretended not to have seen her, and putting on an air of distraction, I poked the rest of the doctor's wig, which had escaped the flames, into the embers with the tongs. I saw then that one of the wrappings around Aspasia's foot was loose. "Allow me," I said, "charming person." So saying, I quickly lowered myself and moved my hands toward the chair where I thought I saw those two legs that great philosophers praised so highly.

I am persuaded that, in this moment, I flirted with a true somnambulism, because my movement was very real, but Rosine, who was lounging on the chair, thought I was moving toward her. Lightly jumping into my arms, she sent the famed shades brought forth by my traveling clothes back to Hell.

Charming country of imagination, you that the charitable Being brought to men to console them for reality, I have to leave you.

It's today that certain people, on whom I depend, pretend to give me my freedom, as if they had taken it from me! As if it was in their power to rob me of it for a single instant and prevent me from traveling to my liking in the vast space always open before me!

They kept me from going about the city, that's true. But they left the entire universe for me; immensity and eternity are at my call.

It's today, then, that I am free, or rather that I will go back into the irons. The yoke of business is going to weigh on me anew. I will no longer take a step that isn't measured by propriety and duty. I'll be happy if some capricious goddess doesn't make me forget both, and if I escape this new and dangerous captivity.

Oh! This means I can't complete my voyage! Was it to punish me that they relegated me to my room? To this delicious land, which enclosed all the good things and all the riches in the world? You might as well wish to exile a mouse in the granary.

However, I have never seen more clearly that I myself am double. While I regret my imaginary joys, I console myself by force. An unseen power follows

me; it tells me that I need air and sky, and that soli-
tude resembles death.

I am ready; my door opens; I roam under the
spacious porticos on the Rue du Po; a thousand
friendly phantoms flutter before my eyes. Yes, here
is this hotel, this door, this stairway; I thrill at going
forward. It's like when you can taste the acid as you
cut into a lemon.

O my beast, my poor jackass, take care of yourself!